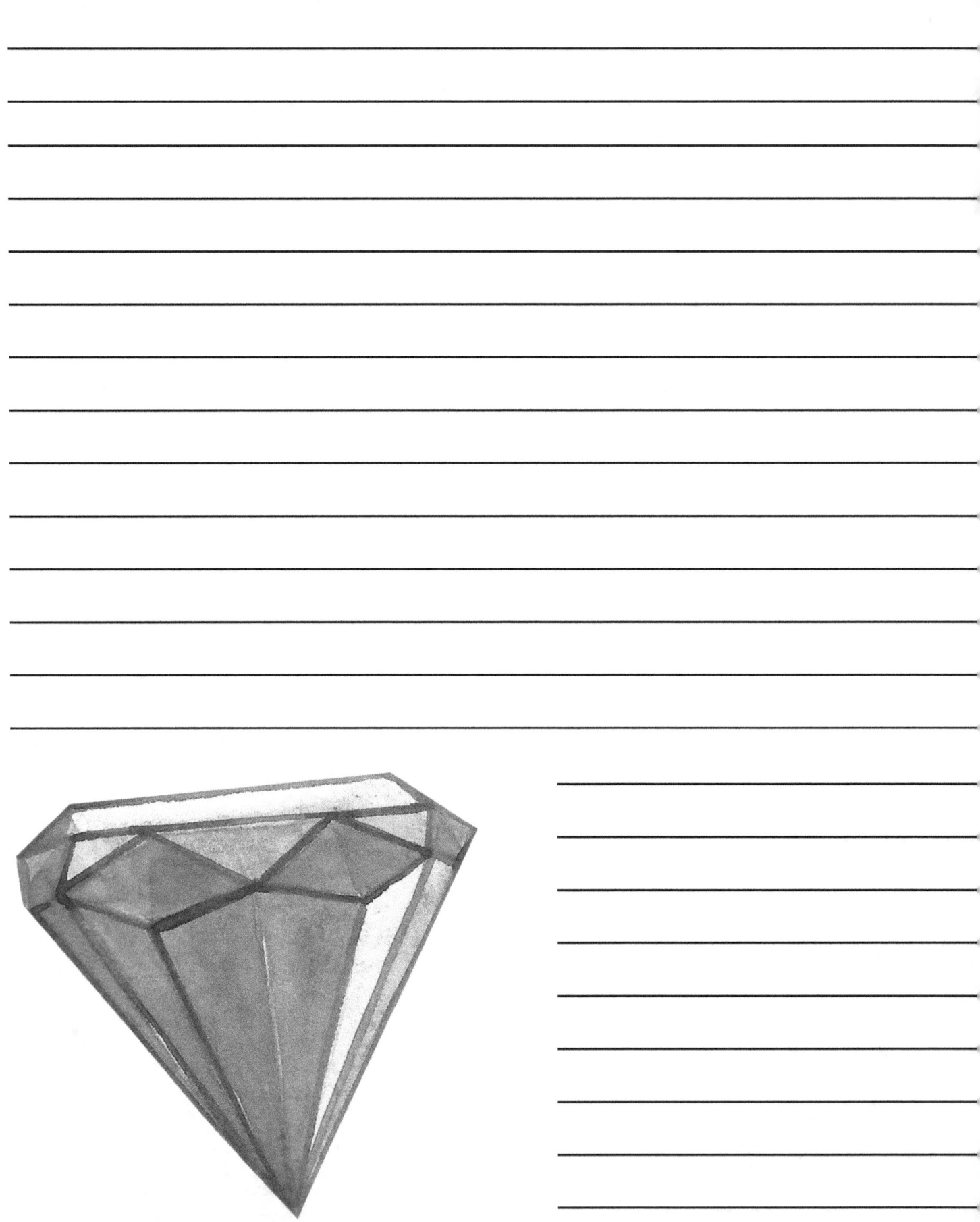

- Acts of Kindness Tracker -

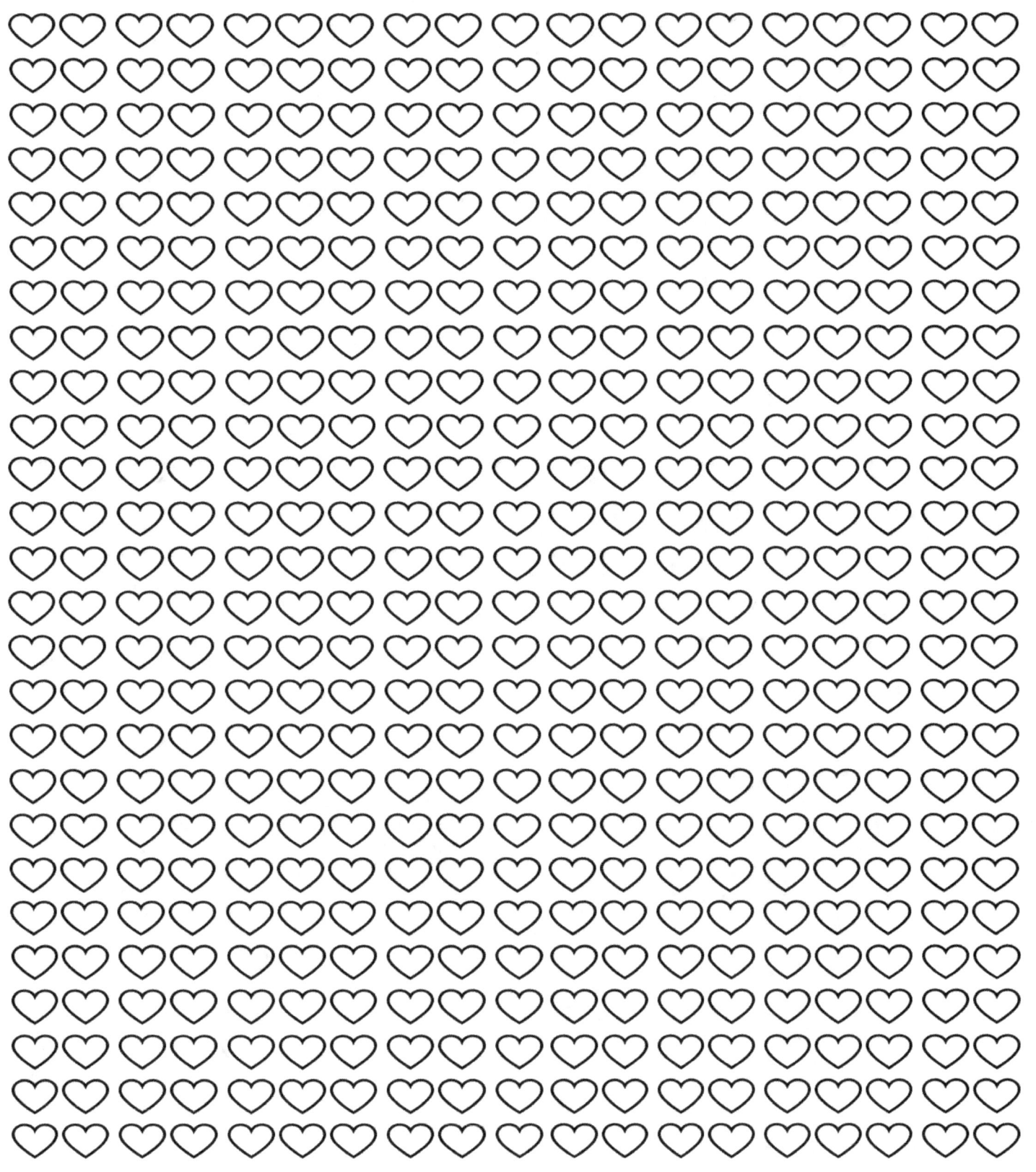

- Acts of Kindness Tracker -

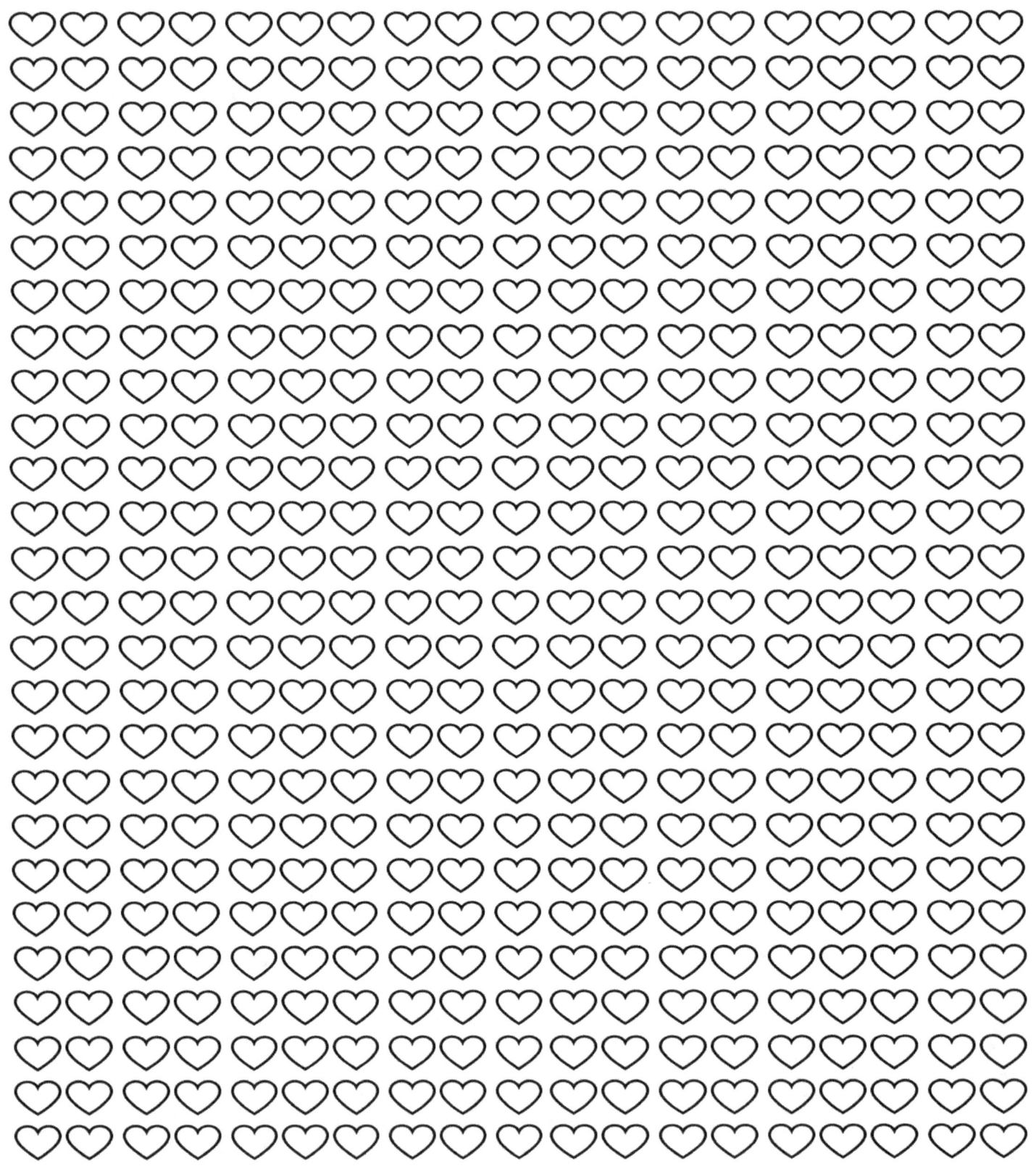

- Acts of Kindness Tracker -

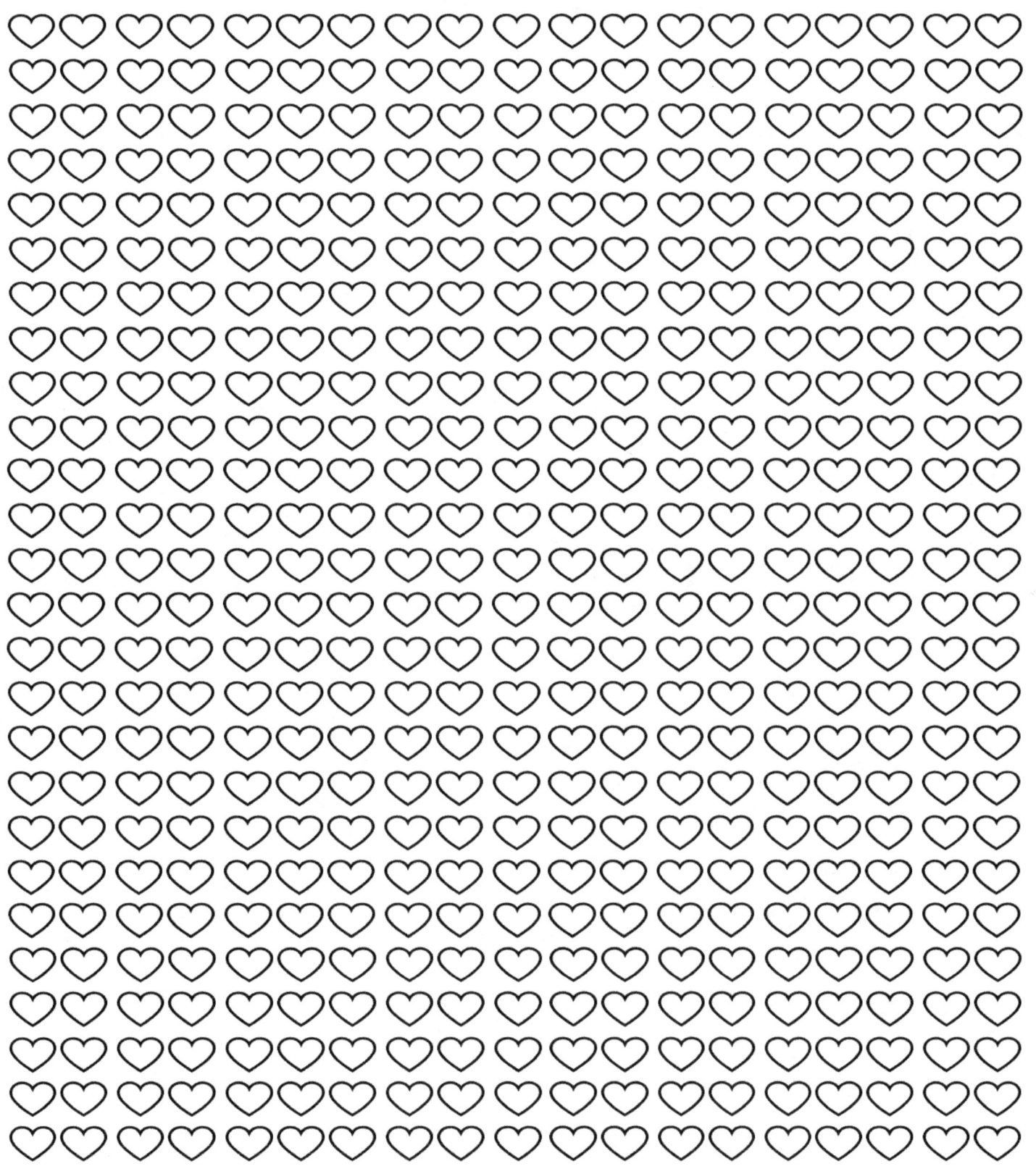

Notes

Notes

Notes

www.ingramcontent.com/pod-product-compliance
Lightning Source LLC
LaVergne TN
LVHW060138080526
838202LV00049B/4020

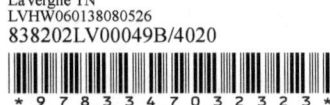